CARING FOR THE PLANET
POLAR REGIONS

Neil Champion

A⁺
Smart Apple Media

Published by Smart Apple Media
2140 Howard Drive West, North Mankato, MN 56003

Design and production by Helen James

Photographs by Alamy (Steve Allen, Brother Luck, Bryan & Cherry Alexander
Photography, Rosemary Calvert, Ashley Cooper, Danita Delimont, George McCallum
Photography, Colin Harris / LightTouch Images, ImageState, Steve Morgan, Peter Arnold,
Inc., Photo Network, Photofusion Picture Library, Robert Harding Picture Library Ltd,
Steve Bloom Images, david tipling, Visual&Written SL, WorldFoto)

Library of Congress Cataloging-in-Publication Data

Champion, Neil.
Polar regions / by Neil Champion.
p. cm. — (Caring for the planet)
Includes biographical references and index.
ISBN-13 : 978-1-58340-512-3
1. Polar regions—Juvenile literature. 2. Endangered ecosystems—Juvenile literature.
I. Title. II. Series.

G587.C45 2004
577'.0911—dc22 2004059196

First Edition

9 8 7 6 5 4 3 2 1

Contents

Earth is an amazing place. It is complex, beautiful, and awe-inspiring. There has been life on it for some three and a half billion years. In all that time, it has grown more complex as life-forms **evolved**. Today, there are more species of plants and animals—about 10 million according to one scientific estimate—and more **habitats** in which they live than at any point in Earth's long history. This is our inheritance. It is this that we are changing at a faster rate than ever before. Our ability to alter the environment to suit our own purposes has never been greater. This allows many of us to live longer, more active lives. These are positive things. However, there are sides to our development and expansion that are not so positive for the planet.

The Polar Biome

Environmental scientists divide the world up into large natural zones called biomes. These biomes include **tundra**, **temperate** woodlands, rain forests, grasslands or prairies, oceans, rivers and wetlands, and deserts. Each biome has a certain type of climate and is characterized by its plant and animal life, which is adapted to live in the conditions it offers.

This book looks at life in the polar regions and the threats they face today. It also looks at some solutions to these threats that may protect what is left of the natural world.

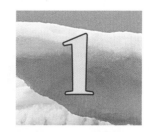

The Polar Deserts

Technically speaking, the frozen, dry polar regions of the world are deserts—cold ones as opposed to the more familiar hot deserts. Polar deserts are found in the far south (Antarctica) and the far north (the Arctic) of our planet. They are defined as places that never get above 50 °F (10 °C) in the summer months and drop well below zero in the winter. Polar deserts are cold for several reasons. They get very little warming energy from the sun, due mainly to their position on Earth. For almost six months of the year, they are immersed in near total darkness, as the sun barely gets over the horizon. This is the polar winter season. During the summer season, a weak sun does shine at a low angle onto the landscape, but because the rays are so spread out, it does not create much heat. Also, because there is so much snow and ice covering the earth, most of the heat and light is reflected back into the atmosphere, a process known as the albedo rate. Snow and ice have a high albedo rating because of their whitish color, which is so reflective that more than three-quarters of the light that hits the polar regions is bounced back again. A grassy field, by comparison, reflects only one-tenth of the total light that hits it. Seen from space, astronauts have reported that Earth is a blue planet due to all of its seas and oceans. At the poles, however, it appears extremely bright because all of this reflected light is sent back into space.

Because polar deserts are so cold, they are incredibly dry. Cold air cannot hold much moisture, which means that very little precipitation falls. In fact, the Antarctic gets less precipitation than the Sahara Desert. There is far less moisture in the interior of the polar regions, as most of the rain and snow the regions do receive falls on the edges of the land, where the sea has more of an effect on the weather.

Antarctic vs. Arctic

The Antarctic and Arctic have very different characteristics. Antarctica, the land surrounding the South Pole, is a continent. It is made up of a landmass that lies inside the Antarctic Circle and is almost totally covered in thick ice. The Arctic, the area surrounding the North Pole, is mostly sea that freezes over, forming **pack ice**. It is made up of the area that lies within the Arctic Circle.

Antarctica

Antarctica is the fifth-largest continent on Earth, almost twice the size of Australia at five and a half million square miles (14 million sq km), and the only continent on which humans have not been able to make their home, if one excludes scientific research stations. It is the most isolated continent, as its nearest neighbor

Antarctic Isolation

A map of Antarctica showing the Antarctic Circle (66° 32' south) and the Antarctic Convergence (around 55° south—see page 15).

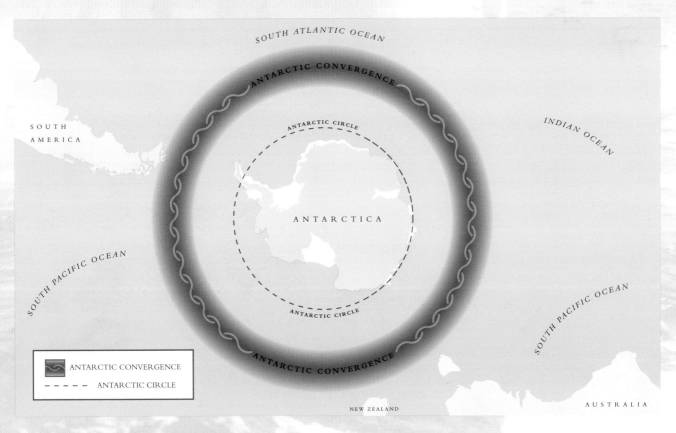

SOUTH ATLANTIC OCEAN

ANTARCTIC CONVERGENCE

ANTARCTIC CIRCLE

INDIAN OCEAN

SOUTH
AMERICA

ANTARCTICA

SOUTH PACIFIC OCEAN

ANTARCTIC CIRCLE

SOUTH PACIFIC OCEAN

ANTARCTIC CONVERGENCE

	ANTARCTIC CONVERGENCE
- - - - -	ANTARCTIC CIRCLE

NEW ZEALAND

AUSTRALIA

Antarctic Icebergs

A tabular iceberg in the Weddell Sea of Antarctica. Up to 80 percent of this mass of floating ice is hidden beneath the water.

Ice Shelves

Huge glaciers formed in the center of Antarctica flow slowly and constantly toward the coast and the sea that surrounds the continent. Where they reach the water, they extend out, forming a shelf of ice still attached to the rocks of the coastline. These ice shelves float on the water, forming a unique type of landscape that makes up about 10 percent of the overall area of Antarctica. The largest is called the Ross Ice Shelf.

is the tip of South America, which is more than 620 miles (1,000 km) away. Antarctica is separated from lands to the north by the stormiest ocean on Earth: the Southern Ocean, which completely surrounds it.

Antarctica is a region of high plateau covered almost entirely in ice that, on average, is well over a mile (1.6 km) thick. Temperatures consistently drop below -40 °F (-40 °C), and winds often blow at more than 185 miles (300 km) per hour in storms that can last for days on end. The center of this vast, ice-bound environment is one of the most extreme places on our planet, more similar to the moon or Mars than to a planet where green things grow and life flourishes. Antarctica is nearly as inhospitable as the bottom of the deep oceans or the summits of the Himalayan Mountains. Only highly adapted organisms stand a chance of surviving here.

Tough Lichen

Lichen growing on a rock on Anvers Island off the Antarctic Peninsula. Lichen is one of the few organisms that can withstand the extreme cold and dark of winter there.

The Antarctic ice sheet is a wonder formed by millions of years of snowfall. It contains about 90 percent of all the ice on Earth, amounting to 7.2 million cubic miles (30 million cu km) in all. Locked in it is a staggering 98 percent of the world's fresh water. If all of this ice melted, the sea level around the world would rise 160 to 200 feet (50–60 m), spelling disaster for life on Earth.

Antarctica is not owned by any country, although seven nations claim part of it: Argentina, Australia, Chile, France, Britain, Norway, and New Zealand. By international **treaty**, it is declared a natural reserve where any nation can carry out peaceful scientific research. In 1991, a 50-year ban was placed upon any form of commercial mining despite the oil, coal, and mineral wealth beneath Antarctica's surface.

A Continent of Extremes

- *Antarctica is the most isolated continent on Earth.*
- *It is the only one not inhabited by the human race, excluding scientific research stations.*
- *It has never witnessed armed conflict.*
- *It is the coldest place on Earth. The record is -129.2 °F (-89.6 °C).*
- *It is the continent with the greatest average height above sea level at 7,500 feet (2,300 m), rising to its highest point of 16,860 feet (5,140 m) at Mount Vinson in the Ellsworth Mountains in a region known as Lesser Antarctica.*
- *It is the windiest continent on the planet.*
- *Its interior makes up the largest and driest desert in the world.*
- *It has the world's largest and longest glacier—the massive Lambert glacier. It is more than 250 miles (400 km) long and 25 miles (40 km) wide. It travels about 0.6 miles (1 km) a year and flows to the sea, where it is more than 125 miles (200 km) wide.*

Hunting Penguins

Adélie penguins hunting from a small iceberg in the cold Antarctic waters. They live and breed on the coastal mainland and islands of the frozen continent.

Antarctic Sea Ice

Also known as pack ice, sea ice forms a permanent ring around Antarctica, attaching the land to the ocean. Sea ice can be 10 to 13 feet (3–4 m) thick. It forms in the frigid winter months and reaches more than seven and a half million square miles (20 million sq km) in area, more than doubling the size of Antarctica. In the summer, when the weather warms the sea, the sea ice shrinks back to one and a half million square miles (4 million sq km). It provides a home for many animals and birds, such as seals and penguins.

Sea ice exerts a major influence on the climate of the region. For example, it keeps Antarctica even colder in the winter by helping to reflect light and heat from the sun. Its presence extends the length of winter and delays the arrival of spring, keeping the whole continent solidly frozen over. It also contributes to the desert-like conditions at the South Pole by keeping the air especially dry. It does this by sealing in the moisture of the unfrozen sea underneath itself. This is one of the reasons that barely any snow—only about one to two inches (2.5–5 cm) a year—falls at the South Pole.

Winter Pack Ice

Pack ice forming in the cold of winter on the surface of the waters around Antarctica. Gulls and skuas take the opportunity to rest.

The Arctic

The Arctic is a region made up mostly of sea (the Arctic Ocean) and pack ice that borders on the landmasses of Alaska, Canada, Scandinavia, and Russia. It includes many large, icy islands, such as Svalbard, which is part of Norway; Baffin Island, which is the largest of the Canadian islands; and Greenland. There is far more variety of life and landscape in the Arctic than in the Antarctic. The climate is warmer and more conducive to plant and animal habitation, especially on islands and the coast of the mainland. The land is characterized in most places by **permafrost** under the surface of the soil. This acts as a barrier that keeps water from draining away. As a result, there is a lot of surface water in the form of lakes, swampy scrub, and tundra.

Around the North Pole itself, the sea is frozen for miles, and very little life is found on the 10-foot-thick (3 m) pack ice. This ice grows in the fall and winter months as cold grips the region, more than doubling the area covered by ice at the North Pole. In the summer, it melts and gives way to more open sea.

Arctic Seas

The Arctic Circle (66° 32' north) defines the region of water that surrounds the North Pole.

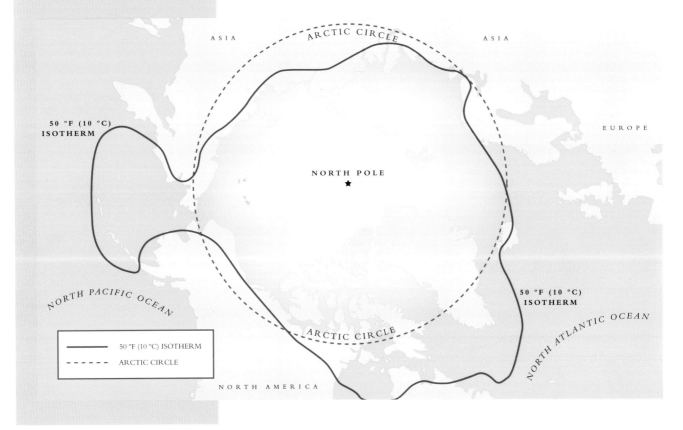

ASIA

ARCTIC CIRCLE

ASIA

50 °F (10 °C)
ISOTHERM

EUROPE

NORTH POLE
★

NORTH PACIFIC OCEAN

50 °F (10 °C)
ISOTHERM

ARCTIC CIRCLE

NORTH ATLANTIC OCEAN

	50 °F (10 °C) ISOTHERM
	ARCTIC CIRCLE

NORTH AMERICA

Life in the Frozen Desert

Life in the north and south polar regions is hard. Winters in both regions see high winds and temperatures well below freezing. The summers are short, and what plants can grow need to make rapid use of the little sunlight available. Animals likewise need to feed and rear young in readiness for the coming cold season. All organisms in these stark land- and seascapes are highly adapted to their environment.

Plants and Animals of the Antarctic

The Antarctic is one of the most inhospitable places on Earth and has one of the simplest **ecosystems**, due to the extreme hostility of its environment. All plants and animals on Earth are made of cells, which contain lots of water. Water—even in cells—turns to ice when the temperature reaches 32 °F (0 °C). Ice takes up more space than water, which means that the cells of living things run the risk of bursting in Antarctica's subzero temperatures. Therefore, only a very few specialized life-forms can survive here. In the continent's frozen interior, only a few **lichens** and **mosses** are able to cope with the intense cold and winter darkness on exposed rocks and mountains. A tiny animal called the mite has also been found here.

In contrast, the ocean that surrounds Antarctica is one of the richest habitats on Earth for marine life. In between these two extremes are many islands and parts of the continent's coastline that are ice-free, although they only amount to two percent of the total coastal area.

Most life at the South Pole limits itself to these islands and coastlines, the ice shelves, the frozen sea, and the water. There are six different types of penguins, many whales (including the minke, the blue whale, and the sperm whale), seals, fish, squid, and visiting seabirds that come to breed in the brief summer months.

The foundation of life in these regions is **zooplankton** and **phytoplankton**. Krill, a type of zooplankton, is the main food of many bigger animals. It has been estimated that there are 660 million tons (600 million t) of krill in the Southern Ocean, forming the main diet of fish, birds, seals, and whales alike. One whale alone can consume up to four and a half tons (4 t) of krill a day. Krill are only available in the summer months when they come closer to the surface, attracted by the sunlight. During this time, they multiply, feeding huge numbers of other animals. However, they disappear into the depths of the ocean in the dark, cold winter months. Therefore, the animals that feed on them either

Shrimp-like Krill

A highly magnified photograph of krill—small, shrimp-like animals that form the diet of many of the larger organisms of the Arctic and Antarctic Oceans.

have to migrate to other waters, as whales and some types of seals do, or endure the winter famine.

The Antarctic Convergence

One of the main reasons that the Southern Ocean is so rich in marine life is the presence of the Antarctic Convergence. It circles the entire Antarctic continent about 500 miles (800 km) off the coast. This 25-mile-wide (40 km) band of water marks the point where the cold currents of water flowing northward from the icy continent meet the warm waters flowing south from the tropics. This produces a very rich region where nutrients well up from the depths of the ocean and provide food for the phytoplankton, which in turn feed krill and other zooplankton, which then feed millions of fish, crabs, whales, and other marine animals. The role of the Antarctic Convergence is vital to the health of the region. The entire ecosystem depends upon it. Threats such as **global warming**, which scientists think could interfere with the complex ocean currents, and an increase in **ultraviolet (UV) radiation**

Penguin Colony

A large colony of king penguins. Penguins are found only in the cold waters and coastal fringes in the southern hemisphere.

Insulation and Other Tactics

Most animals that survive in the deep freeze of the Antarctic do so because they have developed extreme insulation to cope with the conditions. Whales, seals, and penguins have a thick layer of blubber, plus an outer coat of fur or feathers. The Antarctic fur seal has the thickest coat of any animal on Earth.

*Other animals utilize different adaptations to stay warm. The ice fish has hardly any **red blood cells**. This means that its blood is thinner than that of most fish and is easier to pump around its body, keeping it warm. In addition, its heart is twice as large as that of similar-sized fish, helping to pump more of this thin blood.*

Many fish around the coast of Antarctica have a chemical in their bodies that acts like a car's antifreeze, preventing the cells in their bodies from turning to ice in the cold sea temperatures. There is also one type of land animal, the tiny Antarctic mite, that uses this adaptation to stay alive. Instead of freezing at 32 ˚F (0 ˚C), the cells in these animals' bodies can withstand temperatures below 28 ˚F (-2 ˚C).

Huge Seals

Elephant seals on King George island off the tip of the Antarctic Peninsula. These huge animals have thick blubber beneath their skin that keeps them warm.

due to ozone depletion, could have very serious consequences for this life-giving belt of water that circles Antarctica. A general warming of the waters even in these cold regions could alter the mix of waters, their relative temperatures, and their saltiness. These, in turn, could affect the way in which the phytoplankton, the basis of the food chains, behave.

Plants and Animals of the Arctic

The life found on land inside the Arctic Circle is far more complex and abundant than that found inside the Antarctic Circle. This is because there is far more land with vegetation in the Arctic, which gives animals something to eat, meaning that a food chain can be established. Animals that live within the Arctic Circle include polar bears; seals, such as the northern fur seal and the harp seal; walruses; whales, such as the bowhead whale, blue whale, killer whale, beluga whale, and narwhale; Arctic foxes; small mammals, such as the Arctic hare, weasel, and ermine; caribou and moose; and numerous types of seabirds, such as the

Whale Tail
The tail of a humpback whale as it disappears beneath the surface of the ocean. These huge animals live in all of the world's oceans, including the waters around Antarctica.

Snowy Owl

A snowy owl hunting. This bird of the Arctic tundra is found in Alaska, Canada, and Siberia.

Trees and Fossils

Coal has been found on Antarctica, as have the fossils of reptiles that live only in warm climates. These discoveries prove that Antarctica has moved to where it is located today. In fact, it was once part of the southern hemisphere super-continent called Gondwana. This huge landmass was made up of what are today Africa, South America, India, Australia, and Antarctica. But that was 250 million years ago. Around 100 million years ago, Gondwana broke up, and different landmasses moved in different directions. For example, India headed north, where it eventually collided with the landmass of Asia, creating the mighty Himalayan Mountains. Antarctica drifted southward, losing all of its trees, vegetation, and animals as the climate turned colder.

Arctic Fox

Arctic foxes are mammals found in the tundra regions of North America, Europe, and Asia.

18

artic tern, snowy owl, snow goose, and puffin. As in the Antarctic, the basis of the food chain in the sea here is the phytoplankton that bloom in the spring and summer, providing krill and fish with a valuable source of nutrition.

Lord of the Arctic

The polar bear is one of the most majestic and fearsome animals on Earth. It stalks the icy wastes inside the Arctic Circle, looking for seals and other animals that come onto the ice to breed. It is the undisputed lord of the frozen wastes, growing up to 8 feet (2.5 m) tall and weighing 1,300 pounds (600 kg), the largest of all land carnivores. Polar bears have no real natural predators, although humans have the ability to kill them. Pregnant female bears hibernate in dens in the winter to survive the Arctic's extreme conditions. The female bear digs out a home beneath the snow and gives birth while underground. The mothers and offspring then emerge from their den in the spring. Other bears continue to hunt through the long, dark, and cold winter months.

Polar Bear Cubs

A female polar bear with her cubs on the ice of the Arctic wilderness.

The Importance of the Poles

The polar regions are unique and vitally important to the general health of the planet for many reasons. They help provide a balance with the heat generated in the tropics, regulating the climate across the globe. They regulate the all-important ocean currents, keeping nutrients in plentiful supply for marine life. They also provide an environment in which scientists can study Earth's past and work in the least polluted regions of our planet; and they provide the opportunity for different nations to work together on scientific projects on land that is neutral.

Polar regions also provide humanity with a special environment from which to monitor Earth's health. Because they are so sensitive to temperature rises or drops and the effects of pollution, these regions act as an early warning system that can tell us if changes in the global environment are taking place.

The World's Weather

There are around 100 weather stations in Antarctica, some working automatically and others staffed by scientists and technicians. They help monitor weather patterns both regionally and worldwide and enable scientists to gather data on such important phenomena as global warming, **greenhouse gases** in the atmosphere, **cyclones**, and even the occurrence of **El Niño**. They are expensive to maintain and are a measure of

Research Scientists

American scientists at McMurdo Station on Ross Island in Antarctica. A diver is preparing to go underneath the ice.

how important Antarctica is to climate and weather patterns all over our planet.

Antarctica and the stormy Southern Ocean that encircles it are together major players in the global weather system. A massive exchange of energy from the sun takes place in this region and helps regulate the heat balance of the planet as a whole. Hot air from the tropics is cooled over Antarctica. This warm, moist tropical air helps prevent the continent from becoming colder

Storm in Sydney

A thunderstorm over Sydney, Australia. The weather of this part of the world is heavily influenced by the relative closeness of Antarctica.

than it already is, and the cooling of this air by the cold continent in turn helps keep the rest of the world from over-heating. Antarctica actually loses more heat than the sun gives it every year, due partly to the high reflective rate of snow and ice, and only the warm air arriving from the equator helps maintain a balance as this extra heat is used up. The Arctic has a similar, although less dramatic, effect in the northern hemisphere.

Ocean Currents

Antarctica has a big impact on the nutrient-rich currents that flow through the Southern Ocean. In the fall and winter, the cold water beneath Antarctica sinks; in the spring and summer, warming water rises. These temperature differences create moving currents, which are important to the health and **ecology** of the environment because they circulate nutrients and food sources such as plankton. In a similar way, cold water from the Arctic flows south toward the equator and in so doing draws the warm waters of that region northward to replace it. This brings about one of the strongest currents that scientists know of, called the **Gulf Stream**.

Scientific Bases

The frozen continent is used by scientists of many nations for cooperative research into the natural world. Antarctica has no boundaries or fences, although certain nations control different parts, or sectors. There are 37 permanent bases run by 17 different countries. The nations most involved with research are Australia, which has claimed more of the continent (about 42 percent) than any other nation, the U.S., Britain, New Zealand, Russia, Argentina, Chile, Japan, and China. The population in Antarctica's summer months is around 4,000 people, who are distributed across the various research stations. Due to advances in technology and

Antarctic Experiments

These members of the British Antarctic Survey conduct research in one of the harshest environments on Earth.

Solar-heated Station

A scientific station at McMurdo Sound in Antarctica. Solar panels help provide much-needed energy for running the station.

clothing, about 1,000 people live there through the winter as well. The biggest polar base of all is the United States' station at McMurdo Sound on Ross Island in the Ross Sea, which houses up to 1,500 people in the summer.

The almost untouched and relatively unpolluted conditions found in the frozen land around both poles provide scientists with unique opportunities to study world climate, ocean currents, the movements of glaciers, and the formation of icebergs. Additionally, scientists can bore deep into the ice to study the past, just as scientists can study growth rings on the trunk of a tree. Arctic and Antarctic ice has formed over millions of years. Scientists have been able to figure out how old the various layers are, and by studying the formation of the ice and its gas content, they can learn about the climate and general conditions at the time. This work is invaluable to our understanding of Earth's history and ecology.

Scientists also study the **geology** of the regions, looking at the rock formations and piecing together where they came from and what produced them millions of years ago. Monitoring **cosmic rays** to study activity in space is another aspect of scientific life. And, of course, the study of the plants and animals both on land and beneath the Southern and Arctic Oceans is a key part of scientists' work in these regions.

Inuit Builder

Age-old, low-technology solutions to survive nights inside the Arctic Circle. This native Inuit hunter is building an igloo in northwest Greenland out of blocks of snow as his ancestors have done for generations.

Threats in the Wilderness

The vast expanses of Antarctica and the frozen seas around the North Pole still have not been fully explored by people, mainly because of their hostile climates. Thus, these regions are still wilderness areas. But, despite this fact, they are not immune to the effects of humans. Pollution from the industrialized parts of the world has now reached the polar regions. People have exploited their natural resources, and today, even tourism presents a threat in these distant lands.

Pollution in Remote Places

Because the poles are so far from centers of industrial activity, it may seem that their landscapes should remain in pristine condition, untouched by human pollution. However, the sea transports tiny molecules of plastic all around the world, to every remote corner and coastline. The air does a similar thing, carrying minute chemicals from industry and exhaust fumes from vehicles up into the atmosphere and dumping them on glaciers and ice sheets far away. Scientists have recorded these kinds of pollution both on the coast and inland in Antarctica and inside the Arctic Circle.

Exploitation—Oil and Minerals

To date, there has been relatively little exploration by mining and oil companies in the Antarctic. This is mainly due to the extreme remoteness of the continent. The little exploration that has been done has shown that there is oil under the Ross Sea and iron and coal

Oil Spill Victim

A rescue worker holding an almost unrecognizable guillemot, the victim of an oil spill in the seas off the Alaskan coast.

deposits in the mountain ranges. It is believed that there are minerals in Antarctica as well, based on comparisons with similar types of rock that are found in other countries containing minerals.

In the 1950s, the Antarctic Treaty was signed by 12 nations that had an interest in the region. It was designed as an international treaty to protect wildlife, but it was not able to exclude mineral and oil extraction because some of the countries involved wanted to exploit these resources. In 1991, this changed with the establishment of the Madrid Protocol. This agreement states that Antarctica is a natural reserve to be used only for scientific research. All commercial exploitation of the resources found there is banned. The agreement insists that all human activity has to be monitored for its impact on the environment. It also bans any animals not native to the region, which means that dogs, once commonly found at bases, have had to be removed.

Unlike the Antarctic, the Arctic is not highly protected from exploitation for its minerals and fossil fuels. There are several reasons for this. People have always lived on the fringes of the Arctic, and today, almost four million people live in the region. The oil, coal, and minerals inside the Arctic Circle are more accessible than those in Antarctica as well. This makes it very attractive to large energy companies. In Alaska, for example, oil fields cover some 800 square miles (2,000 sq km), and they are expanding. In the far northeastern part of the state lies the Arctic National Wildlife Refuge, a protected region. But local people fear that even this region could be opened up to oil exploration in the future. Because all of the land inside the Arctic Circle is owned by different countries, international environmental concerns often come after the economic needs of individual governments and large, powerful mining and energy companies.

Mining in the Arctic has led to oil spills that have damaged the environment, such as a large oil tanker accident off the Alaskan coast in 1989. Birds such as guillemots, kittiwakes,

Polluting Waste

Pools of oil collect beside these abandoned and leaking oil barrels in Alaska.

28

and divers were killed, as were many sea otters. Alaskan oil fields—as well as their counterparts in Russian Siberia—are a constant threat to the natural heritage of the landscape because of the danger that their pipelines could rupture in the freezing temperatures.

Piping Oil

Oil pipelines in Prudhoe Bay, Alaska. Prospecting for further oil fields in the region has been a controversial subject in recent years.

Exploitation—The Bounty of the Seas

The Arctic Ocean and the Southern Ocean are both full of marine life. Seals, whales, fish, zooplankton, and phytoplankton thrive in these waters. Seal hunting started in the early 19th century, and whale hunting soon followed. People of that time had very little concept of conservation, and large profits were ready to be made from the mass slaughter of these sea animals, hunted for their meat and their oils. Populations plummeted during 150 years of intense hunting.

Fishing has long been common in the northern seas, but heavy fishing in the remote southern seas began fairly late. As stocks of fish around Russian and European waters declined, however, fishing boats ventured farther away from their home ports. Russian ships began commercial fishing of Antarctic cod in the 1960s and were soon taking more than 550,000 tons (500,000 t) of these fish a year from the Southern Ocean. As cod numbers declined, fishermen turned their attention to other types of fish.

Whale Fishing

Crew members on board a Norwegian whaling vessel disposing of the carcass of a Minke whale. Whaling has been heavily regulated in recent years.

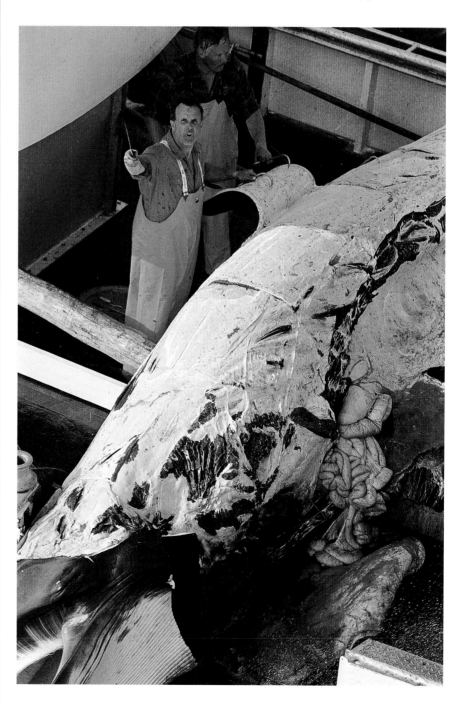

The Blue Whale

The blue whale is the largest animal that has ever lived, making even the largest and mightiest dinosaurs look small by comparison. There were once around 350,000 blue whales swimming the oceans from the Arctic to the Antarctic, feeding in the cooler polar waters in the summer and moving to warmer subtropical waters to breed. However, in the middle of the 19th century, the exploding harpoon was invented. This enabled whalers to kill these huge animals for their valuable oil. By the early 1930s, up to 30,000 blue whales were being killed annually, and by the early 1960s, there were only about 1,000 left. The decline was due solely to humans hunting them to near extinction—99 percent of them were slaughtered by commercial whaling companies. In 1946, the International Whaling Commission was set up with the goal of regulating the number of whales that could be hunted, saving this magnificent animal from almost certain extinction.

*Today, the Southern Ocean has been declared a **marine reserve** where hunting has been banned so that whale populations can slowly increase. One problem that has risen, though, is the high population of crabeater seals in these waters. These animals consume huge amounts of krill, the whales' food. Crabeater seal numbers increased as whale numbers decreased due to hunting. The population of this hungry seal may have to drop before whale numbers can fully increase.*

In the north, a certain number of whales can today be hunted within the Arctic Circle, but this is very regulated. For example, the Inuit have been permitted by the Canadian government to kill one bowhead whale every two years so that their traditional hunting practices can be continued.

Krill were targeted as well, and Russian and Japanese **trawlers** were soon competing with seals, whales, and squid for krill.

When one species, such as the Antarctic cod, krill, or blue whale, is overfished, the delicate balance of the ecosystem is thrown out. Other species may thrive in the absence of a competitor, to the detriment of the ecosystem as a whole. This very serious situation is often difficult to predict, given that the natural world is complex and interrelated. Different species and the environment in which they have developed have achieved a balance over the course of thousands, if not millions, of years. Human interference can disrupt or destroy this balance in only a few years.

Icelandic Cod Fishing: An Example of Overfishing

Cod has long been one of the most important sources of food for people living around the coast of the North Atlantic. Boats have traveled far into the cold waters of the north to make catches of this valuable fish. In the 1970s, fishermen from one of the most prolific fishing nations in the region, Iceland, were catching about 386,000 tons (350,000 t) of cod every year. Today, due to overfishing and a rapid decline in fish stocks, this figure has fallen to less than 220,000 tons (200,000 t) a year—just over half of what was being caught when times were good.

Cod Catch

A catch of cod. This fish has suffered from overfishing, and the population in the North Atlantic is today at an all-time low.

Tourism

Almost any human activity at and around the North and South Poles has some form of negative impact on the environment. Scientific research stations and expeditions create waste products and use energy and chemicals, even when carried out on a very small scale and with great sensitivity. The vehicles used by scientists, on both land and sea, produce small amounts of pollution. Monitoring the breeding habitats of birds and mammals may disrupt their habitats. Merely walking on the fragile mosses and lichens can cause damage that will take 10 years for nature to repair. Although these things are done for the best of reasons—scientific inquiry—they still undermine the fragility of the environment.

Tourism, on the other hand, is done to make profits for companies and to bring pleasure and excitement to those who are paying for the experience. Antarctica has been a destination for wealthy tourists since the 1960s. Still, tourism is not yet a booming business in Antarctica due to the continent's remoteness and danger, as well as the cost of traveling there. Only about 100,000 tourists have ever visited the region, which is equal to or even less than the number that visit famous tourist sites, such as Disney World, Niagara Falls, or Rome, each week. Tourists generally arrive by boat in Antarctica, visit relatively few areas, and go ashore for a very short period of time. Their impact is small, but it is an impact nonetheless. Should tourists be allowed to visit Antarctica? None of the treaties that have been drawn up by governments to protect the continent have ever banned this activity.

Far more tourists get to the Arctic regions. This is mainly because these include parts of mainland Canada and its islands, Alaska, Greenland, and the northern extremes of Norway, Sweden, and Finland. In this situation, the problems of tourism and the fragile Arctic landscape are issues for the individual nations, rather than international treaties, to control.

Tourist Attraction

Tourists in Antarctica can often get very close to penguins such as these emperor penguin chicks.

The WWF International Arctic Program

In 1995, the Worldwide Fund for Nature (WWF) set up a program that would give guidelines to companies that took tourists inside the Arctic Circle. They called it the International Arctic Program. The idea was that both the companies and the tourists who were paying for their services would sign a code of conduct that would minimize the impact of their vacation in this fragile wilderness. The program set out 10 points for Arctic tourism to abide by:

- *Make tourism and conservation compatible.*
- *Support the preservation of wilderness and **biodiversity**.*
- *Use natural resources in a **sustainable** way.*
- *Minimize consumption, waste, and pollution.*
- *Respect local culture.*
- *Respect historic and scientific sites.*
- *Arctic communities should benefit from tourism.*
- *Trained staff members are the key to responsible tourism.*
- *Make your trip an opportunity to learn about the Arctic.*
- *Follow safety rules.*

Responsible Tourism

An ecologically sound way to see the Antarctic coast. These tourists are using double kayaks to paddle around the water between giant icebergs.

Climate Change and the Poles

One of the great questions of our time is whether or not climate change is actually happening. And if it is, is it an entirely natural event, or has the rapid consumption of fossil fuels and increased industrialization over the past 150 years caused it? Or is a combination of natural phenomena and human activities to blame?

Boring Ice

Scientists in Antarctica have managed to drill holes in the ice down to a depth of about one and a half miles (2.5 km). They have extracted ice from the entire length of these holes and have studied the different layers. The deepest ice was laid down about 750,000 years ago, which means that scientists are able to find some clues as to what the climate and atmospheric gases were like from that time to the recent past. Studies of this ice have shown that in the last 750,000 years, our world climate has gone through eight major **ice ages** when the world cooled considerably. In between have been periods of warming when glaciers and ice sheets retreated. Current scientific data indicates that we are entering one of these warming periods now. However, studies have also shown that the current global warming is being intensified by the presence of greenhouse gases that have been put into the atmosphere by human industrial activity over the past 150 years. Study of the ice has shown that levels of these gases were stable until around the start of the **Industrial Revolution** in Europe and America in the 19th century. Since then, levels have risen dramatically. Thus, it seems that we have entered a naturally warm stage in our global climate, but that we will likely see the world get warmer than at any stage in the past 750,000 years due to our production of greenhouse gases. Our planet may become warmer by about 4 °F (2 °C), and scientists have predicted that the temperature increase will be greatest over the poles.

Global Warming and Sea Ice

Studies have recently shown that the Greenland ice sheet is melting at a rate 10 times faster than was previously thought by scientists. The ice sheet is one of the largest in the world, and it has been estimated that if all of the ice contained in this huge expanse were to melt completely, the water that resulted would make the sea level around the world rise by an incredible 23 feet (7 m). This would be enough to drown entire islands in the Pacific Ocean and flood major cities on coasts, including London, New York, and Hong Kong. Early scientific analysis predicted that about 3.3 feet (1 m) of ice would melt off the ice cap every year, but recent studies indicate that a staggering 33 feet (10 m) are disappearing annually. This is due to warmer summers and winters that may be brought on by global warming.

Taking the Temperature

Scientists have found a clever way to keep track of the temperature of the seas around the world. They use an underwater device that sends out long-distance sound waves. These are picked up by receiving stations placed at various points around the world. Sound travels at different speeds based on the average temperature of the water through which it is traveling. By constantly monitoring the speed of sound waves as they travel through the water, scientists can keep a sharp eye on the temperature of our seas and oceans.

Low-lying Islands

The coast of an atoll in the Marshall Islands in the Pacific Ocean. Rising sea levels caused by polar ice melting may affect these and other low-lying areas.

All of this melted ice is fresh water. This means that it dilutes the saltiness of the seas and oceans. Scientists are not sure just what effect this will have. Some fear that a less salty Atlantic Ocean will alter the major ocean currents, such as the Gulf Stream, that move warm water to colder parts of Earth. This would have catastrophic results for the countries of northern Europe and parts of Canada. For instance, the Gulf Stream brings warm water to the west coast of Scotland. Without this extra boost of heat

Cracking Ice

As world temperatures have risen, pieces of continental ice have fallen into the ocean. This huge crack in the ice was photographed on the Larsen Ice Shelf in Antarctica.

from the sea in the winter, this coast would be many degrees colder. This would be a radical change in climate for the people, animals, and plants living in this region, which would mean that species would either migrate away or die out entirely.

The effect may not be quite the same in Antarctica. If global temperatures rise as they are predicted to, the amount of snow falling on the great ice sheet may actually increase. This is because it is the intense cold that keeps the continent dry and desert-like. A little warming may allow the air to hold more moisture and produce increased amounts of snow in the interior.

Global warming may also increase the number and size of icebergs that break off from the ice shelves and float in the sea. Recently, for example, a massive area of ice broke away from the Ross Ice Shelf. Once detached in the ocean, some icebergs float northward into warmer waters and finally melt. This adds to the sea level and changes the salt levels in the ocean.

Less sea ice may form on the oceans in the fall and winter months as well. This means that less heat will be reflected back into the atmosphere because there will be less ice around to reflect it. With more water and less ice, the sea would heat up even more. Once the process of warming starts, it may accelerate rapidly. Because water expands as it gets warmer, this may contribute to a rise in sea levels around the world. If the average sea temperature goes up even slightly, the overall increase in water volume will be significant.

Another result of melting sea ice involves phytoplankton. Sea ice forms one of the most productive areas for phytoplankton growth during the spring and summer bloom. Less sea ice would likely mean less phytoplankton for the fish, whales, seals, and squid that rely on them for food, either directly or indirectly.

A Hole in the Ozone

Ozone is a naturally occurring gas found high up in the **stratosphere**, a part of the atmosphere located between 8 and 30 miles (12–50 km) above Earth's surface. The **ozone layer** within the stratosphere surrounds the planet and helps protect us from some of the sun's harmful UV rays. These rays can cause skin cancer in humans and may have a harmful effect on other animals and even crops. This means that even though there is only a tiny amount of ozone in our atmosphere, it plays a very important role in protecting life on Earth.

In the natural course of things, ozone remains at a fairly stable quantity—about 0.00004 percent—in our atmosphere. However, scientists noticed in 1981 that there appeared to be a "thinning" of the gas over Antarctica. Scientists set out to find the reasons behind this. They tracked the cause to a group of chemicals known as CFCs (chlorofluorocarbons) manufactured by industries and used in such products as refrigerators, air conditioners, and aerosol sprays. Over the years, millions of tons of CFCs had been pumped into the air by people all over the world. Levels had reached a point high enough that they reacted with the ozone and destroyed some of it—up to 30 percent over Antarctica and 2.5 percent worldwide. The result was that great quantities of harmful UV radiation were getting through our atmosphere.

These increased rays are believed to be responsible for an increase in skin cancer in countries such as Australia in recent decades.

Increased quantities of UV radiation hitting Earth's surface may also have an adverse effect on the Antarctic food chain because these rays slow the rate of **photosynthesis**. All creatures in the Southern Ocean depend on phytoplankton multiplying in huge quantities. Krill and other zooplankton feed on the plants, and they, in turn, feed bigger animals in the ocean. If there is a decrease in the ocean's plant life, all other sea creatures, great and small, will suffer.

Damaging Fumes

Greenhouse gases rising in great plumes from the stacks of a power plant.

In 1987, the world community began trying to do something about the plight of the ozone layer. The main goal was to reduce the quantity of CFC gases we use in products such as hairsprays, in hopes that the ozone layer would regain its normal protective thickness in the upper atmosphere. There are ongoing studies to monitor just how effective this has been. However, it may take a long time to reverse the damage done by decades of CFC emissions.

6

Protecting the Future

For almost 50 years, the nations of the world have been working together to protect the Antarctic. International treaties and agreements safeguard this fragile environment and its plants and animals. Large-scale efforts to protect the Arctic have been undertaken as well, but it will take the continued care of nations and individuals to protect the unique polar habitats into the future.

The Antarctic Treaty

The Antarctic Treaty, signed in 1959, states that "it is in the interest of all mankind that Antarctica shall continue to be used forever for peaceful purposes and shall not become the scene or object of international discord." So far, the treaty has held up. This international agreement has protected the continent from exploitation, such as drilling for oil or mineral extraction. It defines Antarctica as a natural reserve. There are no purely military bases on the continent, although the militaries of several nations, including the U.S., maintain a presence. Weapons development and testing are strictly banned.

Protecting Plants and Animals

Since 1972, seals in Antarctica have been protected by international agreement. Throughout the 19th century, fur seals were hunted mercilessly for commercial gain. Their numbers fell dramatically, as nearly 3 million were killed over a period of 150 years. Today, there is no

commercial hunting of seals in the Southern Ocean or on the ice of Antarctica. The numbers of fur seals have slowly risen as a direct result.

Humpback, minke, and blue whales were all hunted almost to extinction; well over one million whales were slaughtered in the seas around Antarctica throughout the 20th century. In 1994, Antarctica was declared a whale sanctuary, although the Japanese still kill a few minke whales each year for scientific purposes.

In 1982, life in the Southern Ocean received further protection by the Convention on the Conservation of Antarctic Marine Living Resources, an international charter. This charter did not consider just those individual species that were suffering due to overfishing or hunting; it looked at the interdependence of all species in the environment and called for the protection of the whole. This approach was quite new and has proved to be highly successful. Commercial fishing and hunting still take place in the region, but strict quotas have been set up to allow stocks of fish and krill to be maintained or even increased. The goal is sustainable use of resources. Scientists are now monitoring animals that are not traditionally caught or hunted to see how

Protected Seals

A southern fur seal in Antarctica. These animals are now protected from commercial hunting under an international treaty.

species that are harvested affect their numbers. The goal is to improve our understanding of how the ecosystem works. This means understanding how the complex interactions between living organisms, the waters of the oceans, the rocks of the land, and the climate of the region work together to create its unique habitats. As data is compiled, it is used to make further policies.

The Great Arctic Reserve

A very recent development has been the creation of the Great Arctic Reserve, which is located on the Taimyr Peninsula in Siberia in northern Russia. It is one of the largest areas of protected land in the world, covering more than 17,760 square miles (46,000 sq km). The World Wide Fund for Nature helped the Russian government create it. The reserve is home to much Arctic wildlife, including polar bears, seals, and almost 750,000 reindeer. The region is monitored, and hunting and other forms of exploitation of the natural landscape are prohibited.

Greenpeace

The Greenpeace ship Esperanza docked in the Norwegian Arctic. It was there to draw attention to the damage done by oil tankers in the region.

Conservation Organizations

There are many organizations, both national and international, that monitor life in fragile and endangered habitats around the world, including polar regions. They help to ensure that these environments will survive long into the future. Here are some of the more well-known ones:

• **Friends of the Earth**   www.foe.org
Founded in 1971 in Britain, Friends of the Earth is now one of the world's best-known and most respected environmental pressure groups.
• **World Wide Fund for Nature (WWF)**   www.panda.org
Founded in 1961, this Swiss-based organization raises money to fund conservation operations around the world, focusing in particular on endangered animals.
• **Greenpeace**   www.greenpeace.org/usa/
Founded in 1971 in Canada, Greenpeace has grown to become one of the world's biggest and most influential environmental pressure groups. It campaigns all over the world on behalf of the environment.
• **International Union for the Conservation of Nature (IUCN)**   www.iucn.org
This organization publishes books listing all of the world's endangered animals and habitats. These books present the most comprehensive picture we have of the state of the planet in terms of threats to species.

What You Can Do to Help

The poles are a long way from the places most of us call home. They are among the most difficult and dangerous regions on Earth to try to reach. Stormy seas, strong winds, and freezing temperatures have all taken their toll on the brave explorers and scientists, past and present, who have ventured to the extremes of our planet. However, that does not mean that we should ignore the polar regions or the problems they face in the 21st century. There are many ways in which we can involve ourselves with the life of the polar regions, because our actions directly affect the state of our world. Here are just a few examples of what you might do:

• Get involved with helping to raise people's awareness of the fragile polar environments. This can be done through school projects or by joining a club involved with the natural world.

• Get involved at school to find out more about the fascinating lives of polar animals, both on land and in the sea.

• Help and support environmental organizations dedicated to protecting polar regions. Fund-raising events and awareness days can be fun to take part in.

• In delicate and beautiful natural environments, take nothing but photographs and leave nothing but footprints. That way, you will always leave the wild places that are left on Earth in the same state in which you found them.

Further Reading

Conaln, Kathy. *Under the Ice*. Toronto: Kids Can Press, 2002.

Crossley, Louise. *Explore Antarctica*. New York: Cambridge University Press, 1995.

Mason, Paul. *Polar Regions*. North Mankato, Minn.: Smart Apple Media, 2005.

Rootes, David. *The Polar Regions*. Philadelphia: Chelsea House, 2001.

Scott, Elaine. *Poles Apart*. New York: Viking, 2004.

Woodford, Chris. *Arctic Tundra and Polar Deserts*. Austin, Tex.: Raintree Steck-Vaughn, 2002.

Web sites

Antarctica: Scientific Journey from McMurdo to the Pole
http://www.exploratorium.edu/origins/antarctica/index.html

Arctic Studies Center
http://www.mnh.si.edu/arctic

NOAA Arctic Theme Page
http://www.arctic.noaa.gov/index.shtml

Secrets of the Ice
http://www.secretsoftheice.org

The Seventh Continent
http://penguincentral.com/penguincentral.html

Virtual Tour: Antarctica
http://astro.uchicago.edu/cara/vtour

Glossary

Biodiversity The numbers and types of different plants and animals living in a specific environment.

Cosmic rays Streams of high-energy particles that constantly bombard Earth from outer space.

Cyclones Very powerful winds that can develop in the atmosphere when the pressure is very low.

Ecology The study of living organisms and their relationships with the environment.

Ecosystems Natural units of the environment in which all of the plants, animals, and nonliving components depend on each other in complex ways.

El Niño An event that occurs around Christmas every five to eight years in the Pacific Ocean off South America, in which an irregular warm swell of ocean replaces the normally cold-water currents.

Evolution A theory which claims that all life has come from single-celled forms and has slowly become more complex.

Geology The study of Earth, its history, and structure, and the makeup of all of the rocks in its landscape.

Global warming The process by which Earth's climate is thought to be getting warmer through an increase in greenhouse gases.

Greenhouse gases Gases, including carbon dioxide and methane, that trap heat in Earth's atmosphere.

Gulf Stream A warm ocean current that originates in the Gulf of Mexico and flows north past the east coast of North America, then heads east across the Atlantic around Newfoundland.

Habitats Parts of an environment that are self-contained, supplying the needs of the organisms that live within them.

Ice ages Periods in Earth's history during which the average temperature drops, producing a climate in which glaciers grow in the long, cold winters.

Industrial Revolution The movement from an agricultural society to one based on industrial products. This process began in Britain in the mid-18th century and spread to other European countries and the U.S.

Lichens Life-forms that consist of a specific fungus and alga combined together. They grow on rocks and trees and can survive harsh conditions.

Marine reserve   An area of sea or ocean that is protected by international law from fishing, whaling, and dumping.

Mosses   Plants that do not have any flowers. There are more than 10,000 different species around the world.

Ozone layer   Ozone is a form of oxygen that forms in Earth's upper atmosphere. The ozone layer protects our planet from some of the harmful ultraviolet rays from the sun.

Pack ice   Areas of ice that form on cold seas around the Arctic and Antarctic. Winds blow smaller areas of pack ice together to form much larger sections floating on the sea. (Also known as sea ice.)

Permafrost   Permanently frozen soil found just below the surface of the ground. It is associated with the tundra regions of northern Russia and Scandinavia and is also found high up in mountain ranges.

Photosynthesis   The process by which green plants on land and in the oceans turn sunlight and carbon dioxide from the atmosphere into oxygen and food for themselves.

Phytoplankton   A general name given to the many different types of microscopic plants that live in the oceans.

Red blood cells   Cells in the blood that carry oxygen around the body.

Stratosphere   A layer within Earth's atmosphere. It starts at about 8 miles (12 km) high and extends to about 30 miles (50 km) high, and contains the ozone layer.

Sustainable   Something that can be carried out indefinitely into the future.

Temperate   A term used to describe a climate that is neither too hot nor too cold. Temperate zones are found halfway between the hot tropics and the cold poles.

Trawlers   Fishing vessels that use a large net, which they drag along behind them to scoop up fish.

Treaty   An agreement by two or more parties that is written down and becomes legally binding.

Tundra   Land close to or inside the Arctic Circle, where the layer of soil just below the surface is permanently frozen due to year-round low temperatures.

Ultraviolet (UV) radiation   Part of the range of radiation that is given off by the sun. Humans cannot see it with the naked eye. It causes sunburn and skin cancer.

Zooplankton   A general name given to the many types of tiny animals that float in the oceans and seas, including krill.

Index